QUEEN BEE

CHYNNA CLUGSTON

An imprint of

📖 SCHOLASTIC

New York   Toronto   London   Auckland   Sydney   Mexico City   New Delhi   Hong Kong   Buenos Aires

To my favorite art teacher, Mr. Zimmerman.
Thank you for the encouragement, Mr. Z. Rest in peace.

C.M.

Fort Miller Middle School, Fresno, CA

Lyrics excerpted from: "The Beat," © The Go-Go's, *Beauty and The Beat*,
IRS Records/A&M. All rights reserved.

4

THEN, AS LUCK WOULD HAVE IT, MY BODY DECIDED TO PLAY A REALLY MEAN TRICK ON ME...

REMAIN... CALM...!

IT WENT TOTALLY CRAZY, AND I DON'T JUST MEAN THE NORMAL STUFF THAT HAPPENS TO GIRLS, EITHER—I MEAN, I HAD SOMETHING *EXTRA*-WEIRD GOING ON.

SHRIEK!

SMASH

WHEN I WAS TOO LAZY TO REACH FOR THE REMOTE CONTROL, IT WOULD JUST UP AND *FLOAT OVER* TO ME...

THAT'S WHEN I KNEW SOMETHING PRETTY FREAKY WAS GOING ON.

VWWWP

THINGS STARTED RANDOMLY FLYING AROUND OR BREAKING WHEN I WAS REALLY UPSET.

ONE MORNING I EVEN MANAGED TO LET THE CAT IN THE DOOR WITHOUT GETTING UP FROM THE KITCHEN TABLE!

MEOW?

FLAKES!

I WAS WORRIED, SO I TOLD MY MOM WHAT WAS HAPPENING TO ME. SHE TOLD ME I HAD INHERITED THE GIFT OF *PSYCHOKINESIS*, THE ABILITY TO MOVE INANIMATE OR FARAWAY OBJECTS WITH MY MIND.

"*GIFT?!*" MORE LIKE A CURSE!

5

I THOUGHT AT ANY MOMENT I'D START HEARING UNCLE BEN FROM SPIDER-MAN TELLING ME THAT "WITH GREAT POWER COMES GREAT RESPONSIBILITY!" I WAS FREAKING OUT! WHY DID I HAVE TO GET SOME LAME, SUPERHUMAN KIND OF POWER?

WHY COULDN'T I JUST BE *NORMAL*?

HONEY, *"NORMAL"* DOESN'T EXIST. JUST DON'T WORRY ABOUT IT SO MUCH, OKAY?

Y-YEAH...

WHY COULDN'T I TIME TRAVEL OR DISAPEAR OR FLY OR SOMETHING? ALL I COULD DO WAS MOVE STUPID STUFF AROUND WITH MY MIND!

WELL, OF COURSE *PSYCHOKINESIS* JUST ADDED TO MY PROBLEMS AT SCHOOL. I COULDN'T CONTROL IT AT ALL, SO I TRIED TO HIDE IT. I THOUGHT IF I IGNORED THE POWER IT'D GO AWAY. YEAH, RIGHT!

I MADE A COUPLE ATTEMPTS TO HANG WITH THE POPULAR GIRLS OR AT LEAST TALK TO THEM, BUT SOMETHING DUMB WOULD ALWAYS HAPPEN.

HALEY, *YOU* COME OVER HERE.

ALL RIGHT!

I HEARD YOU COULD PLAY SOFTBALL PRETTY WELL, SO DON'T LET ME DOWN, OKAY?

I WON'T!

6

8

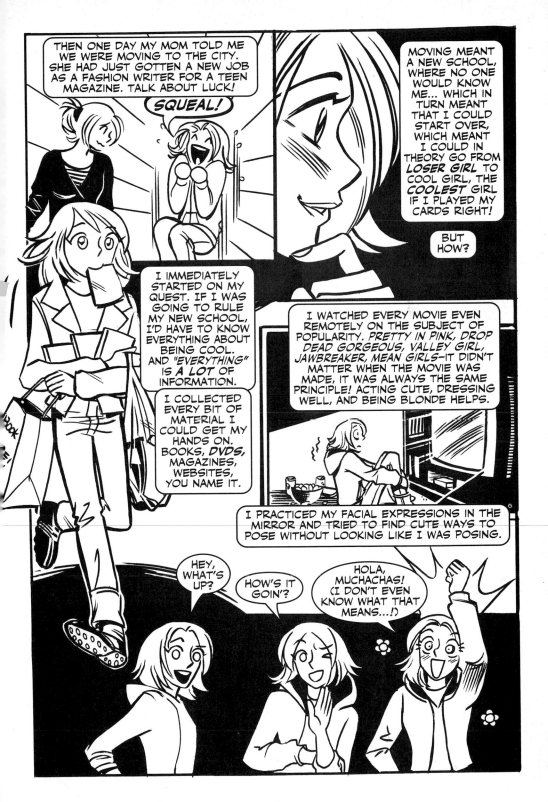

THEN ONE DAY MY MOM TOLD ME WE WERE MOVING TO THE CITY. SHE HAD JUST GOTTEN A NEW JOB AS A FASHION WRITER FOR A TEEN MAGAZINE. TALK ABOUT LUCK!

SQUEAL!

MOVING MEANT A NEW SCHOOL, WHERE NO ONE WOULD KNOW ME... WHICH IN TURN MEANT THAT I COULD START OVER, WHICH MEANT I COULD IN THEORY GO FROM *LOSER GIRL* TO COOL GIRL, THE *COOLEST* GIRL IF I PLAYED MY CARDS RIGHT!

BUT HOW?

I IMMEDIATELY STARTED ON MY QUEST. IF I WAS GOING TO RULE MY NEW SCHOOL, I'D HAVE TO KNOW EVERYTHING ABOUT BEING COOL. AND "EVERYTHING" IS *A LOT* OF INFORMATION.

I COLLECTED EVERY BIT OF MATERIAL I COULD GET MY HANDS ON. BOOKS, *DVDS*, MAGAZINES, WEBSITES, YOU NAME IT.

I WATCHED EVERY MOVIE EVEN REMOTELY ON THE SUBJECT OF POPULARITY. *PRETTY IN PINK, DROP DEAD GORGEOUS, VALLEY GIRL, JAWBREAKER, MEAN GIRLS*—IT DIDN'T MATTER WHEN THE MOVIE WAS MADE, IT WAS ALWAYS THE SAME PRINCIPLE! ACTING CUTE, DRESSING WELL, AND BEING BLONDE HELPS.

I PRACTICED MY FACIAL EXPRESSIONS IN THE MIRROR AND TRIED TO FIND CUTE WAYS TO POSE WITHOUT LOOKING LIKE I WAS POSING.

HEY, WHAT'S UP?

HOW'S IT GOIN'?

HOLA, MUCHACHAS! (I DON'T EVEN KNOW WHAT THAT MEANS...!)

I WEEDED THROUGH MY WARDROBE AND MADE SURE ALL OF LAST YEAR'S FASHIONS TOOK A PERMANENT VACATION.

UGH! I ACTUALLY *WORE* THIS?!

I KEPT UP ON MY CELEBRITY GOSSIP AND PUMPED MY MOM EVERY FEW DAYS TO SEE WHAT WAS NEW IN THE FASHION WORLD THAT I MIGHT HAVE MISSED.

MOM, ANYTHING?

IF YOU ASK ME AGAIN THIS WEEK, I'M GOING TO TOSS YOUR LAPTOP OUT THE WINDOW.

OKAY THEN, THAT'S A DEFINITE "NO."

THERE WAS SO MUCH TO DO BEFORE MY GRAND ENTRY INTO A NEW SCHOOL. I PROBABLY WOULDN'T HAVE SLEPT AT ALL IF I DIDN'T KNOW IT'D GIVE ME BAGS UNDER MY EYES. BUT AFTER SEVERAL WEEKS OF CAREFUL PLANNING, I WAS READY.

NO MORE "MOUSEY GIRL!" NO MORE PATHETIC LUNCH HOURS SITTING BY MYSELF, FRIENDLESS AND MISERABLE! MY DAYS OF *GEEKDOM* ARE *OVER!*

I'M GONNA BE *THE MOST POPULAR GIRL* AT *JOHN F. KENNEDY INTERMEDIATE SCHOOL* AND NOTHING IS GOING TO STOP ME!!!

THE NEXT DAY.

...AND AS I'M SURE YOU'VE ALREADY NOTICED, WE HAVE A NEW STUDENT JOINING US TODAY.

HER NAME IS HALEY MADISON, AND SHE'S A TRANSFER STUDENT FROM--

LOOK FRIENDLY, LOOK CUTE, LOOK COOL... DON'T GRIN TOO MUCH, THEY CAN SMELL A GEEK A MILE AWAY.

APPARENTLY MS. MADISON HAS NOT BEEN SHOWN AROUND THE SCHOOL AS OF YET, SO I THINK IT WOULD BE NICE TO HAVE A VOLUNTEER SHOW HER THE ROPES. WITHIN A REASONABLE AMOUNT OF TIME, OF COURSE.

I DON'T WANT ANY OF YOU TAKING AN HOUR AND A HALF TO GO HANG OUT NEXT TO THE SODA MACHINE.

ME!

ME!

OOO, I WANT OUT OF CLASS!

ON SECOND THOUGHT, I THINK THE VOLUNTEER SHOULD SHOW HALEY AROUND DURING LUNCH.

SHOOM

YOU GUYS ARE SO PREDICTABLE! COME ON, HANDS UP. WHO WOULD LIKE TO SHOW HALEY AROUND SCHOOL DURING LUNCH?

HA HA HA!

PLEASE LET SOMEONE RAISE A HAND!

11

THIS IS TRINI TURNER, HALEY. YOU'RE IN GOOD HANDS WITH HER.

HEY.

WELCOME TO JFK! IT'S PROBABLY NOT TOO DIFFERENT FROM THE SCHOOL YOU WENT TO BEFORE THIS, WITH ONE EXCEPTION:

JFK HAS SOME SIMPLY AMAZING PEOPLE WHO GO HERE.

MYSELF, FOR EXAMPLE.

I SEE!

JUST KIDDIN'. BUT I DO HAVE TO SAY THERE ARE SOME REAL CHARACTERS HANGING AROUND! LET ME INTRODUCE YOU TO MY CREW.

WE HANG OUT NEXT TO THE LIBRARY. IT'S SORT OF THE "BRAIN-SLASH-OTAKU-SLASH-GOTH" AREA, JUST SO YOU KNOW. WE DON'T ALL HANG OUT ALL THE TIME OR ANYTHING, BUT WE CAN DEAL WITH EACH OTHER BETTER THAN IF WE HAD TO SIT NEAR THE FOOTBALL GUYS OR THE PARTY KIDS.

YEAH.

HEY, GUYS, MEET HALEY.

HI, HALEY!

HEY!

HALEY, THIS IS PAIGE.

'SUP?

PAIGE IS A GOOD TIME... SHE'S OUR CLASS VICE-PRESIDENT, AND TOTALLY OBSESSED WITH TOP OF THE CHARTS MUSIC, WHICH EXPLAINS HER FUNNY-LOOKING EARS.

THEY'RE ACTUALLY HEADPHONES THAT HAVE BEEN THERE SO LONG, THEY'VE MOLDED TO HER HEAD.

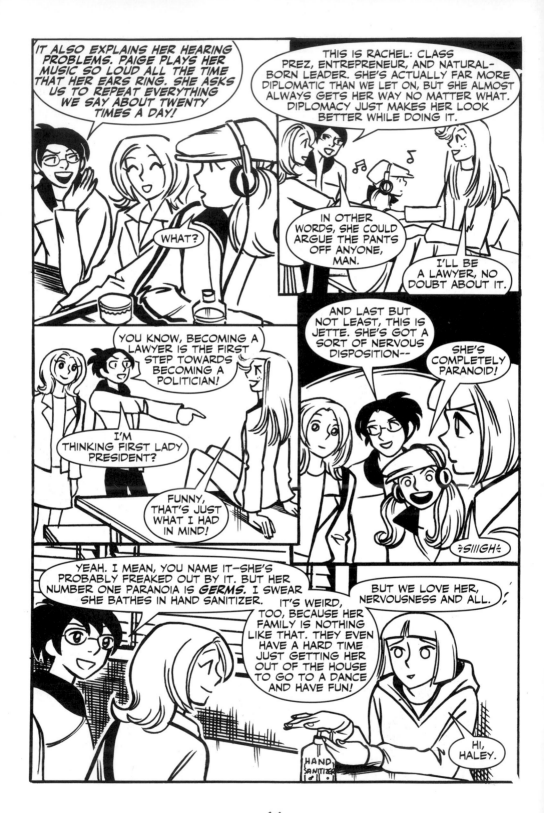

IT ALSO EXPLAINS HER HEARING PROBLEMS. PAIGE PLAYS HER MUSIC SO LOUD ALL THE TIME THAT HER EARS RING. SHE ASKS US TO REPEAT EVERYTHING WE SAY ABOUT TWENTY TIMES A DAY!

WHAT?

THIS IS RACHEL: CLASS PREZ, ENTREPRENEUR, AND NATURAL-BORN LEADER. SHE'S ACTUALLY FAR MORE DIPLOMATIC THAN WE LET ON, BUT SHE ALMOST ALWAYS GETS HER WAY NO MATTER WHAT. DIPLOMACY JUST MAKES HER LOOK BETTER WHILE DOING IT.

IN OTHER WORDS, SHE COULD ARGUE THE PANTS OFF ANYONE, MAN.

I'LL BE A LAWYER, NO DOUBT ABOUT IT.

YOU KNOW, BECOMING A LAWYER IS THE FIRST STEP TOWARDS BECOMING A POLITICIAN!

I'M THINKING FIRST LADY PRESIDENT?

FUNNY, THAT'S JUST WHAT I HAD IN MIND!

AND LAST BUT NOT LEAST, THIS IS JETTE. SHE'S GOT A SORT OF NERVOUS DISPOSITION--

SHE'S COMPLETELY PARANOID!

≈SIIIGH≈

YEAH. I MEAN, YOU NAME IT—SHE'S PROBABLY FREAKED OUT BY IT. BUT HER NUMBER ONE PARANOIA IS *GERMS*. I SWEAR SHE BATHES IN HAND SANITIZER.

IT'S WEIRD, TOO, BECAUSE HER FAMILY IS NOTHING LIKE THAT. THEY EVEN HAVE A HARD TIME JUST GETTING HER OUT OF THE HOUSE TO GO TO A DANCE AND HAVE FUN!

BUT WE LOVE HER, NERVOUSNESS AND ALL.

HAND SANITIZER

HI, HALEY.

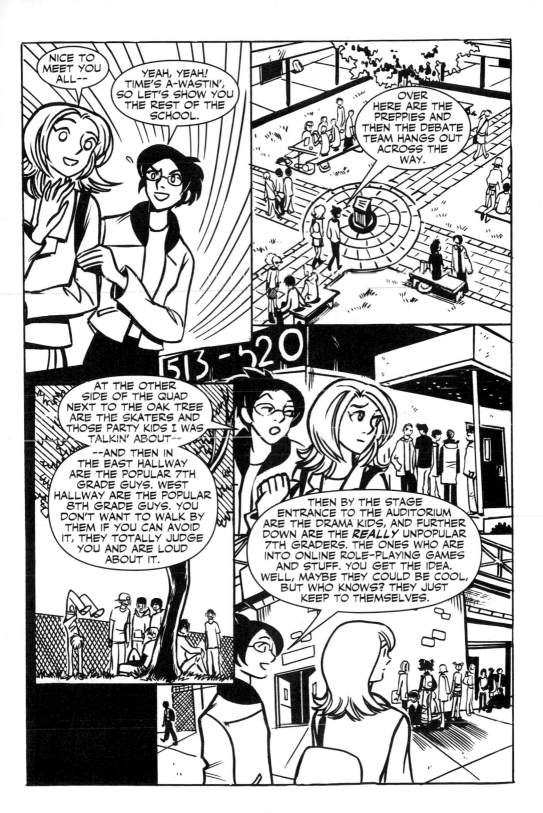

I NEEDED TO FIND A WAY TO STAND OUT SO THAT THE HIVE WOULD SEE ME AS SOMEONE THEY'D WANT IN THEIR GROUP, AND FAST. OTHERWISE I'D JUST BE STUCK HANGING OUT WITH TRINI AND HER FRIENDS. NO HOPE OF SUPERPOPULARITY THERE.

THE PROBLEM WAS THAT I COULDN'T FIGURE OUT WHAT KIND OF AMAZING THINGS WOULD GET THAT HIVE BUZZING. UNTIL AFTER SCHOOL...

WHAT'S WRONG?

SOME 7TH GRADER GRABBED MY SNEAKER WHEN I WAS TRYING TO PUT IT ON AND THREW IT INTO THAT TREE! THERE'S NO WAY I CAN GET IT BACK DOWN... AND NOW MY MOM'S GONNA KILL ME! I'LL BE GROUNDED UNTIL I'M EIGHTEEN...

I SEE WHAT YOU MEAN!

WHY DON'T YOU GO WASH OFF YOUR FACE AND I'LL TRY TO GET IT DOWN FOR YOU, OKAY?

'KAY...

UUUHN!

LET'S GO!

HOW'D YOU *DO* THAT?!

WHOA! DID YOU *SEE* THAT?

AFTER THAT, THE WHOLE SCHOOL KNEW WHO I WAS. WORD ABOUT MY RESCUE AND LIGHTENING-QUICK MOVES SPREAD FAST VIA IMS AND CELLS. SUDDENLY I'M EVERYBODY'S HERO. EVEN THE 8TH GRADERS ARE IMPRESSED: THEY HATED THAT BULLY, TOO.

THE WHOLE SCHOOL KNEW ABOUT ME NOW... SO DID *THE HIVE.*

...OKAY. SO WHAT DO YOU GUYS THINK ABOUT THAT NEW GIRL?

WELL, SHE HAS REALLY GOOD CLOTHES, AND EVERYONE SEEMS TO LIKE HER...

I HEARD HER MOM IS, LIKE, SOME *BIG FASHION MAGAZINE* BOSS OR SOMETHING. THAT COULD BE SUCH AN IN TO WHAT'S GOING TO BE ON THE RACKS BEFORE THE NEWS EVEN HITS THE GLOSSIES!

WHAT DO *YOU* THINK ANJIE?

COOL! WELL, IN THAT CASE, MY FRIENDS AND I WERE WONDERING IF YOU'D LIKE TO HANG WITH US TOMORROW. I WOULD SAY TODAY, BUT LUNCH IS ALMOST OVER, AND WE BELIEVE IN ALWAYS STARTING AFRESH WITH THE FULL LUNCH HOUR WHEN WE'RE *INTERVI* -- ER, MEETING NEW PEOPLE.

SOUNDS GOOD. SEE YOU TOMORROW!

NEEDLESS TO SAY, I WAS COMPLETELY PREPARED FOR ANY QUESTIONS THEY ASKED ME. THEIR INTERVIEW WENT SOMETHING LIKE:

SHOES, HAIR PRODUCTS, FAVORITE COLORS, MUSIC, AND MOVIES.

SKIN CARE, MAKEUP, BRA SIZE, BOYS, JEANS, MINISKIRTS, AND BRACELETS.

SO HERE I AM, ALL SETTLED INTO THE HIVE. THERE'S ONLY ONE PROBLEM: MY *PSYCHOKINESIS* STILL GOES PSYCHO SOMETIMES!

AND WHATEVER HAPPENS ALWAYS MAKES ANJELICA LOOK BAD, EVEN THOUGH IT'S TOTALLY NOT MY FAULT!

WAS THAT A BAG OF CHIPS ON HER BACK?

MUST BE A LITTLE STATIC ELECTRICITY IN THE AIR TODAY, TOO.

ZZZAP

AAA!

MUST BE A LOT OF... UH... MOISTURE IN THE AIR TODAY!

SO I'M EXCLUSIVELY HANGING OUT WITH *THE HIVE* NOW, AND EVERYTHING IS GOING ACCORDING TO PLAN. ANJIE HAS STOPPED COMPETING WITH ME ENTIRELY, AND NOW ALL THE GIRLS LOOK TO ME FOR ADVICE. MY OPINION ENDS UP BEING THE FINAL WORD ON EVERYTHING, AND IN THEORY, THIS SHOULD BE GREAT... EXCEPT I DON'T FEEL EXACTLY THE WAY I THOUGHT I WOULD.

I'M BEGINNING TO WONDER IF TRINI WAS ACTUALLY RIGHT: MAYBE I DON'T BELONG IN THIS HIVE.

12:05

LOOK AT HER. THAT GIRL'S BUTT IS WAY TOO BIG FOR THOSE JEANS.

I DON'T EVEN KNOW WHY SAMANTHA PUTS ON MAKEUP. HER SKIN LOOKS LIKE THE SURFACE OF THE MOON! SHE'LL NEVER BE ABLE TO COVER IT ALL UP!

LOOK AT SANDY! THAT GIRL TOTALLY DRESSES LIKE A RETIRED SPICE GIRL!

12:22

I CAN'T BELIEVE YOU THINK TAD IS CUTE. HIS HAIR LOOKS LIKE HE GOES AROUND STICKING FORKS IN POWER SOCKETS!

HOLD UP, HERE COMES THAT WITCH, CAROLINE.

HA HA HA

29

EVERYBODY IS TOTALLY IN LOVE WITH *ALEXA*. EVEN *ANJIE* THINKS SHE'S GREAT. IT'S ALL ALEXA, ALL THE TIME...ALEXA, ALEXA, ALEXA. I'M JUST, LIKE, "WHATEVER."

BUT EVEN THOUGH I THOUGHT ALEXA WAS A TOTAL SOCIAL FAKER, I WAS STILL PRETTY EXCITED THAT THERE WAS SOMEONE ELSE AT SCHOOL WITH *PSYCHOKINETIC* ABILITIES, YOU KNOW? MAYBE WE COULD BE "PSYCHO" TOGETHER OR SOMETHING. *HA!*

HALEY, IS IT? CAN I TALK TO YOU FOR A SECOND IN MY OFFICE?

SO, YOU'VE GOT IT TOO, HUH? THAT HURRICANE IN CLASS YESTERDAY? I'VE NEVER HAD THAT HAPPEN BEFORE. YOU KNOW WHAT I'M TALKING ABOUT, RIGHT?

UH, YEAH...I DO! WOW, IT'S SO NICE TO FINALLY MEET SOMEONE WITH THE SAME--

YEAH, WHATEVER. LISTEN, I THINK IT *MIGHT* BE A WISE IDEA IF WE MADE SURE STUFF LIKE THAT DIDN'T HAPPEN AGAIN, YOU KNOW? IT CAN'T BE TOO HARD FOR YOU TO CONTROL YOURSELF, IF I CAN DO IT. BUT MAYBE FOR SAFETY'S SAKE, YOU SHOULD STAY OUT OF MY WAY...SO NO ONE GETS *HURT*.

OH, RIGHT... SURE.

AFTER ALL, WE DON'T WANT TO ATTRACT THE *WRONG* KIND OF ATTENTION, DO WE? THOUGHT NOT.

45

GETTING OVER-EMOTIONAL AGAIN. MUST CALM DOWN BEFORE--

SMASH

≥SIGH≥ TOO LATE.

OKAY, SO MAYBE THE TEXT MESSAGE WAS A MISTAKE. NO MATTER WHAT ALEXA DID TO GET ME IN TROUBLE IN THE FIRST PLACE, NO ONE *KNEW* ABOUT IT!

I SHOULD HAVE BEEN MORE CAREFUL.... OF *COURSE* EVERYONE WOULD *SUSPECT ME* WHETHER THE CALLER ID WAS BLOCKED OR NOT. I'M THE ONLY ONE WHO WAS MORE POPULAR THAN ALEXA WAS BECOMING, THE ONLY ONE WHO COULD BE REALLY THREATENED BY HER.

SOB!

THIS IS *SO* LAME. I DON'T KNOW WHAT TO DO TO WIN EVERYONE BACK... WHAT *CAN I* DO? THERE'S NOTHING! NOTHING! IT'S GONNA BE NERDSVILLE AGAIN FOR ME. ARGGH.

46

EITHER WAY, I NEED TO TRY TO GET MY GRADE IN SOCIAL STUDIES BACK UP. IF ONLY I COULD GET MRS. GERSTINE TO LET ME TAKE A MAKEUP TEST!

I CAN'T DO IT, HALEY.

PLEASE? I WANT TO MAKE THIS RIGHT, MRS. GERSTINE. HOW CAN I PROVE I WASN'T TRYING TO CHEAT OTHER THAN BY TAKING A MAKEUP TEST ON THE SAME SUBJECT?

THAT WOULDN'T WORK, EITHER. I CAN'T CHANGE YOUR F NOW.... AT THIS POINT, IT MIGHT AS WELL BE SET IN STONE. I'M SORRY.

I-I UNDERSTAND... I'LL JUST HAVE TO FLUNK OUT OF SCHOOL, I GUESS... GET A PART-TIME JOB OR TWO TO SUPPORT MYSELF... EAT INSTANT RAMEN NOODLES FOR THE REST OF MY LIFE. MAYBE A CHEESE-BURGER ON HOLIDAYS, IF I'M LUCKY...

LOOK, HALEY, IF YOU WANT TO BRING YOUR GRADE BACK TO WHERE IT WAS, WHAT YOU REALLY NEED TO DO IS ACE THIS REPORT COMING UP. WE TALKED ABOUT IT AFTER THE TEST.

THERE'S ONE CATCH, THOUGH -- IT'S NOT A SOLO PROJECT. YOU NEED TO WORK WITH A PARTNER.

YES. WELL, ONE YOU'LL GET ALONG WITH. I HAVE YOU SET TO WORK WITH... JASPER REINES.

WHO?

A PARTNER?

JASPER REINES... THE QUIETEST BOY IN THE 7TH GRADE. I HADN'T REALLY NOTICED HIM BEFORE, NOW THAT I THINK OF IT.

THAT'S HIM IN THE BACK OF THE CLASS THERE. GO AHEAD AND TAKE A SEAT NEXT TO HIM TODAY, SINCE WE'LL BE STARTING TO BRAINSTORM ON REPORT SUBJECTS.

47

HELLLLLO, HALEY. LOOKING FOR ANYTHING IN PARTICULAR?

GAH!

UM, NOT ESPECIALLY...

REALLY. THEN YOU AREN'T LOOKING FOR AN ENSEMBLE TO WEAR FOR A CERTAIN TALENT SHOW? BECAUSE A LITTLE BIRDIE TOLD ME THAT, LIKE MYSELF, YOU WERE GOING TO COMPETE IN THE AMER-I-CAN DREAM CONTEST!

NOPE, I'M JUST...SHOPPING FOR SCHOOL CLOTHES....

JUST SHOPPING, EH? THAT MUST MEAN YOU ALREADY HAVE YOUR COSTUME FOR THE CONTEST, RIGHT? SO THEN, WHAT'S THAT YOU HAVE IN YOUR HANDS?

...'CAUSE IT SURE IS ADORABLE! IT'S A LITTLE TOO MUCH FOR SCHOOL. MAYBE I'LL BUY MYSELF THE SAME ONE FOR THE CONTEST.

B-BUT YOU CAN'T!

I-I MEAN, WHAT IF I WAS THINKING OF BUYING IT? YOU WOULDN'T WANT THE SAME WARDROBE AS ME, WOULD YOU?

DANG! I TOTALLY THOUGHT THIS MIGHT BE THE OUTFIT TO GET, TOO!

WELL, IF I'M ONLY WEARING IT FOR THE CONTEST, IT SHOULDN'T BE A PROBLEM SHOULD IT? I WEAR MINE ONCE, AND YOU CAN WEAR YOURS FOR THE REST OF THE YEAR!

WELL, I SHOULD GET GOING... GOTTA MEET MY MOM IN A LITTLE WHILE!

SEE YOU AROUND.

59

I HAVE TO ASK YOU, THOUGH... WHY DO YOU WANT TO HANG OUT WITH ANJELICA AND *THE HIVE* INSTEAD OF GIRLS LIKE TRINI AND HER FRIENDS? YOU GOT ALONG WITH THEM BETTER, FROM WHAT I SAW.

UM... WELL...

I-I FOUND OUT THAT TRINI WASN'T AS NICE AS SHE SEEMED. SOMEONE TOLD ME THAT SHE WAS REALLY JEALOUS ALL THE TIME AND STARTED ACTING ALL WEIRD AND SAYING MEAN STUFF ABOUT ANYONE THAT ANJIE TRIED TO HANG OUT WITH.

"SOMEONE" TOLD YOU THAT? DID YOU EVEN THINK ABOUT WHY THEY MIGHT BE TELLING YOU THAT KIND OF STUFF?

YEAH, I MEAN... WELL, I DIDN'T THINK SHE'D LIE TO ME ABOUT SOMETHING LIKE THAT. I THOUGHT SHE WAS MY FRIEND.

IT WASN'T?

NO! TRINI'S REALLY NICE. NOT FAKE NICE, BUT ACTUALLY NICE.

SOUNDS LIKE A LOUSY FRIEND, 'CAUSE IT WASN'T LIKE THAT AT ALL!

ONE OF MY SISTERS KNEW TRINI BACK IN GRAMMAR SCHOOL AND SAYS SHE WASN'T A JEALOUS TYPE AT ALL. ANJIE STOPPED HANGING OUT WITH HER BECAUSE TRINI WASN'T AS *"COOL LOOKING"* AS THE OTHER GIRLS.

ANJIE NEVER CARED HOW TRINI FELT; SHE WAS ALL ABOUT *"BEING POPULAR"* AND LAME STUFF LIKE THAT. TRINI ONLY SEEMED CLINGY BECAUSE SHE DIDN'T WANT TO LOSE HER BEST FRIEND, BUT SHE GAVE UP AFTER ANJIE MADE FUN OF HER IN FRONT OF EVERYONE ON THE PLAYGROUND ONE DAY.

AND THAT'S HOW THAT STUPID RUMOR GOT OUT.

GEEZ...

ANJIE THOUGHT SHE'D NEVER BE POPULAR IN THE 7TH GRADE HERSELF IF THEY KEPT ON BEING FRIENDS.

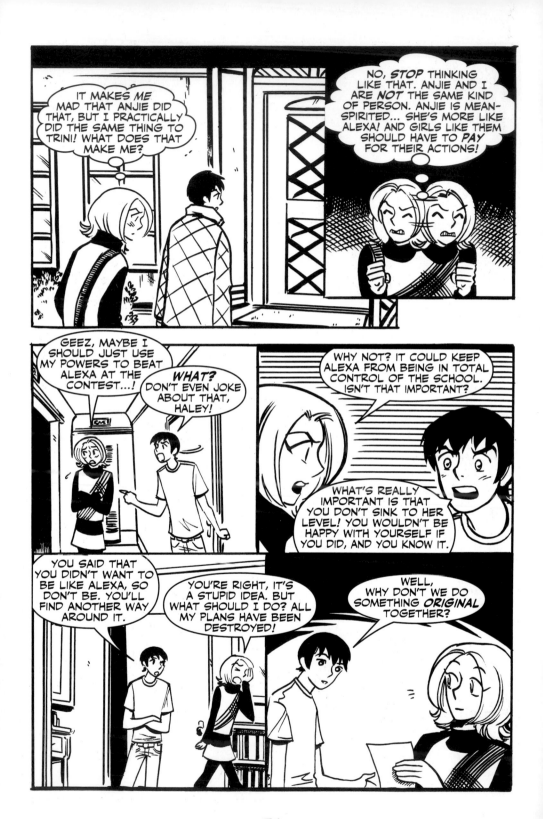

THANKS TO JASPER, THE QUESTION OF WHAT TO DO FOR THE COMPETITION WAS SOLVED. BUT ONE BIG PROBLEM STILL REMAINED:

WHAT WAS I GOING TO DO ABOUT THE ALEXA INCIDENT?

"HALEY, HOW COULD YOU?!"

HEE-HEE

THE FACT WAS THAT JASPER, ALEXA, AND I ALL KNEW I DIDN'T ACTUALLY THROW THE TRAY.

BUT, WE ALSO KNEW THAT THERE WAS NO WAY TO PROVE THAT I DIDN'T, EITHER. I WAS STUCK LOOKING LIKE THE BAD GUY.

WELCOME TO THE FIRST EVER *AMER-I-CAN* DREAM CONTEST!

YAMMER YAMMER YAMMER

WE HAVE COMPETITORS FROM ALL OVER THE COUNTY HERE TONIGHT, AND AN *AWESOME* SHOW TO PRESENT TO YOU...

OH, GEEZ -- I CAN'T BELIEVE HOW NERVOUS I AM!

...SO LET'S PUMP THEM UP! I WANNA HEAR SOME *NOISE* BEFORE WE BEGIN!

WOOOOO! CLAP CLAP CLAP

DON'T WORRY ABOUT IT -- YOU'RE GOING TO BE *GREAT*.

I'M NOT WORRIED ABOUT THE ACT, I'M WORRIED ABOUT WHAT KIND OF TRICKS ALEXA IS GOING TO TRY TO PULL WHILE WE'RE ONSTAGE!

EVERYONE, EVERYONE--

I JUST WANTED TO TELL EVERYONE, FROM THE BOTTOM OF MY HEART: *BREAK A LEG,* AS THEY SAY IN SHOW BIZ!

AW!

THANKS, ALEXA!

SAME TO YOU!

SHE'S SO *SWEET!*

"SHOW BIZ" MY EYE! SHE MEANS IT LITERALLY!

I WOULDN'T JUST WORRY FOR *OUR* SAFETY, THAT'S FOR SURE.

KIND OF GIVES YOU THE CREEPS, DOESN'T IT?

103

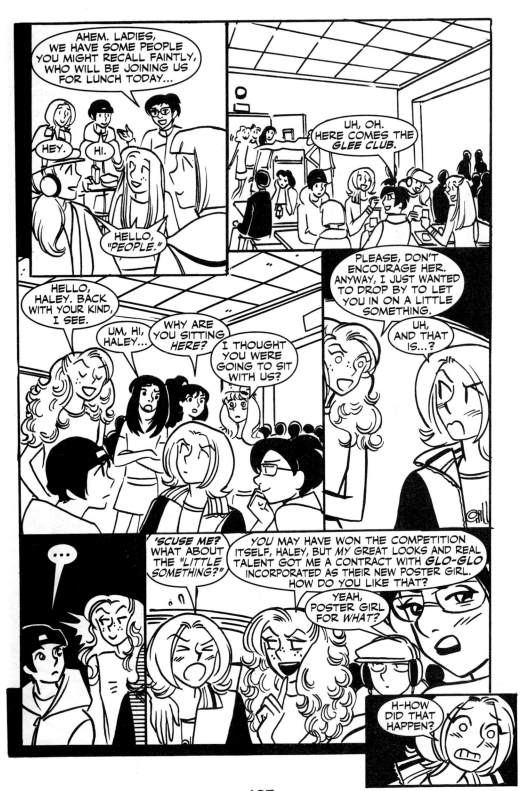

AHEM. LADIES, WE HAVE SOME PEOPLE YOU MIGHT RECALL FAINTLY, WHO WILL BE JOINING US FOR LUNCH TODAY...

HEY.

HI.

HELLO, "PEOPLE."

UH, OH. HERE COMES THE *GLEE CLUB.*

HELLO, HALEY. BACK WITH YOUR KIND, I SEE.

UM, HI, HALEY...

WHY ARE YOU SITTING *HERE?*

I THOUGHT YOU WERE GOING TO SIT WITH US?

PLEASE, DON'T ENCOURAGE HER. ANYWAY, I JUST WANTED TO DROP BY TO LET YOU IN ON A LITTLE SOMETHING.

UH, AND THAT IS...?

'SCUSE ME? WHAT ABOUT THE *"LITTLE SOMETHING?"*

YOU MAY HAVE WON THE COMPETITION ITSELF, HALEY, BUT *MY* GREAT LOOKS AND REAL TALENT GOT ME A CONTRACT WITH *GLO-GLO* INCORPORATED AS THEIR NEW POSTER GIRL. HOW DO YOU LIKE THAT?

YEAH, POSTER GIRL FOR *WHAT?*

H-HOW DID THAT HAPPEN?

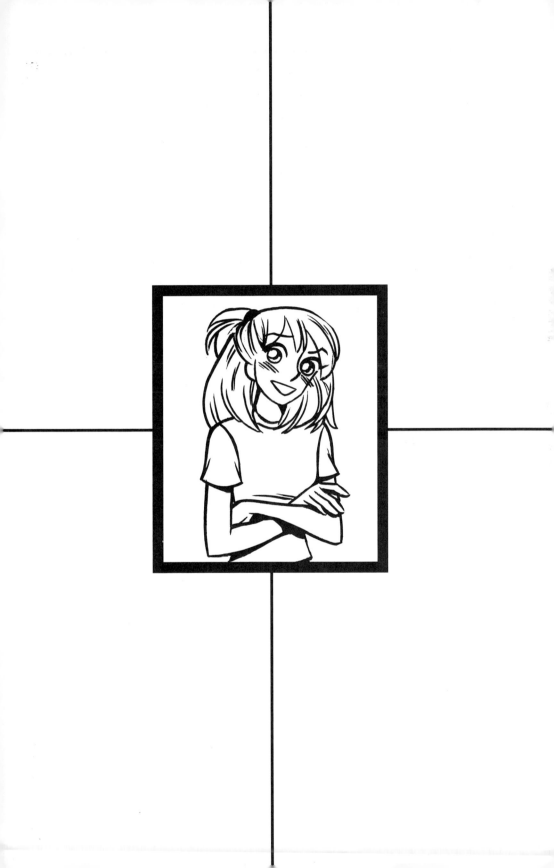

Only one Queen Bee
can rule the middle school hive...
and guess who's still stinging!!??!!

Alexa knows a secret . . .
and Haley is in for a big surprise!

Check out the following pages for a hint about what's next in
Queen Bee, the supercool graphic novel series by Chynna Clugston.

GET THE BUZZ! Look for news on *Queen Bee* and all our other exciting
Scholastic Graphix books. Log on to www.scholastic.com/graphix

An imprint of
SCHOLASTIC